D1441154

Out of Water Otter

Written and Illustrated by
Dakota Daetwiler

Dedicated to my son, Jett.
With special thanks to Jane DeHaan.

Visit us on the web at:
www.alta.lib.ia.us
or call (712) 200-1250
to renew your books!

About the Author

Dakota Daetwiler is a 26 year old artist, gallery owner, author, and entrepreneur. She has a lot of passion for creating and inspiring in any way possible. Daetwiler was born and raised in Fortuna, California; where she currently resides and operates her gallery "Dakota's Designs." She loves taking trips the nearby town of Trinidad, and has painted scenery from it many times. This book's illustrations are based on the look and feel of Trinidad's beautiful beaches.

If you would like to check out her work please visit her gallery in Fortuna, or visit any of her websites listed below.

If you would like to have this book autographed please contact her anytime! She loves meeting kids and encouraging them to follow their dreams.

www.PaintingsByDakota.com
www.facebook.com/DakotasDesigns
Twitter: @DakotasDesigns
Instagram: @DakotasDesigns
Email: DakotasDesigns@hotmail.com

Dakota's Designs Art Gallery
1040 Main Street
Fortuna, CA 95540

There once lived an otter
who loved all things green.
He explored the mountains,
the hills and the trees.

He fearlessly ran and played
all through the land,
But when it came to water
he would stop at the sand.

When the water would touch the little otter's toe,
He would imagine the things that were deep down below.

They were big, they were mean, they were anything but fun,
So back to the land the little otter would run!

Sometimes the otter would sit all
alone at the docks,
And watch as the other otters
jumped off the rocks.

They would yell and they would
play, but mostly they would say,
"Come in, Little Otter, the water
is great today!"

"No way! No Way!" the little otter would say.
"Too many scary monsters live in that bay!"

As he answered the little otter
peered over the side,
But he couldn't see in the water no
matter how he tried.

He was concentrating so hard he
didn't even notice,
Behind him up crept his little
brother Otis!

With one hard PUSH the little otter fell in.
Then something strange happened, he started to swim!

The little otter swam with eyes very wide.
There really were no monsters under the tide!

He dove and he splashed, then swam to the floor.
There was so much to see, he was scared no more!

For the next several hours
the otter had a blast,
The ocean was beautiful,
colorful, and vast.

When they were all done swimming in the deep blue sea,

Little Otter proclaimed, "It's time to come with me!"

Little Otter hurried to land and
shook his fur dry.
The other otters wouldn't follow,
he didn't know why.

"We've heard there are lots of
scary monsters out there!"
So instead of coming up, they
just gave him a stare.

"Come on you scaredy otters,
there's lots to explore!
The ocean is great but it's more
fun on the shore!"

The little otter then showed his
brothers the land,
The mountains and trees and
squishy warm sand.

They all learned a lot that adventurous day.
They learned that new things weren't as bad as they say.

And from then on all the otters knew
Not to let fear tell them what to do!

There is fun to be had and great stuff to see.
Trying new things really is the key!

And so they played on from the sea to the land,
Overjoyed thinking of the adventures at hand.

The End

33743896R00021

Made in the USA
San Bernardino, CA
09 May 2016